SAM SHEPARD

• *A Particle* •
of Dread

Sam Shepard is the Pulitzer Prize–winning author of fifty-five plays and three story collections. As an actor, he has appeared in more than sixty films and received an Oscar nomination in 1984 for *The Right Stuff*. He was a finalist for the W. H. Smith Literary Award for his story collection *Great Dream of Heaven*. In 2012, he was awarded an honorary doctorate from Trinity College, Dublin, Ireland. He is a member of the American Academy of Arts and Letters, received the Gold Medal for Drama from the Academy, and has been inducted into the American Theater Hall of Fame. He lives in New York and Kentucky.

• A Particle •
of Dread

SAM SHEPARD

A Particle · of Dread

of Dread

A PLAY

Vintage Books

A DIVISION OF PENGUIN RANDOM HOUSE LLC

NEW YORK

A VINTAGE BOOKS ORIGINAL, MARCH 2017

Copyright © 2017 by Sam Shepard

Library of Congress Cataloging-in-Publication Data
Names: Shepard, Sam, 1943– author. | Sophocles. Oedipus Rex.
Title: A particle of dread : a play / by Sam Shepard.
Description: Vintage Books original. |
New York : Vintage Books, 2017.
Identifiers: LCCN 2016036184 (print) | LCCN 2016047844 (ebook) |
ISBN 9781101974391 (softcover : acid-free paper) |
ISBN 9781101974407 (ebook)
Subjects: LCSH: Oedipus (Greek mythological figure)—Drama. |
BISAC: DRAMA / American. | FICTION / Literary.
Classification: LCC PS3569.H394 P37 2017 (print) | LCC PS3569.H394
(ebook) | DDC 812/.54—dc23
LC record available at https://lccn.loc.gov/2016036184

Vintage Books Trade Paperback ISBN: 978-1-101-97439-1
eBook ISBN: 978-1-101-97440-7

www.vintagebooks.com

Printed in the United States of America
10 9 8 7 6 5 4 3 2 1

• A Particle •
of Dread

The world premiere of A *Particle of Dread* was originally produced by Field Day at the Playhouse, Derry, Ireland, and opened on November 30, 2013. It was directed by Nancy Meckler; the set design was by Frank Conway; the costume design was by Lorna Marie Mugan; the lighting design was by John Comiskey; the sound design was by Sam Jackson; the production manager was Lisa Mahony; and the stage manager was Clare Howe. The original cast was as follows:

OEDIPUS/OTTO	Stephen Rea
UNCLE DEL/TRAVELER/TIRESIAS	Lloyd Hutchinson
LAIUS/LAWRENCE/LARRY/LANGOS	Frank Laverty
JOCASTA/JOCELYN	Bríd Brennan
OFFICER HARRINGTON	Iarla McGowan
FORENSIC INVESTIGATOR R. J. RANDOLPH	Caolán Byrne
MANIAC OF THE OUTSKIRTS	Lloyd Hutchinson
ANTIGONE/ANNALEE	Judith Roddy

Scene 1

OPENING: (*No preset music or anything to indicate what's up ahead other than empty stage. White light up on* OEDIPUS, *center stage in black-striped bib overalls, short-sleeved white T-shirt, black janitor shoes. His left foot is much larger than his right. He walks with an exaggerated limp.* OEDIPUS *is mopping up blood from the stage floor. The blood is dripping down from his eyebrows, but* OEDIPUS *pays no attention to its origins; he just keeps mopping up the constant flow of blood as he speaks.*)

OEDIPUS: This . . . this was the place, wasn't it? Roads, trees. Right here. Isn't this the place where you held me down? Your foot on my back. My chest in the mud. Here, wasn't it? Someone—someone held me while you hammered a steel spike right through my ankle. Yes, that was it! A spike! Flash of light. Your powerful arm. Every inch of blood. Every vein. My ankle remembers. (*Pause.*) Or no— Was this the place you dropped me off? Could've been. Draped in mystery and confusion. The secret let out. Maybe that was it.

Full of fear as you were. Trembling, running, hauling me across your back. Flapping like an extra skin. You think I'd forget? Your breath, panting like a bull calf born. Day and night. Leaves and wind. Left for dead. Hanging from an olive tree. A baby human. Left for dead.

(OEDIPUS *exits. Lights shift.*)

Scene 2

(*Downstage center sits* UNCLE DEL *on a stool: a large muscular man in a white butcher's apron splattered with blood, rubber boots, long-sleeved plaid shirt open over white T-shirt, sleeves rolled up. He's digging his hands into large metal bucket in front of him, coming up with bleeding animal skins, dripping blood and streaming water. He wrings them out while listening to* LAWRENCE, *who is pacing left and right, downstage of* DEL, *in a dark three-piece suit and overcoat, daubing his sweaty face with white handkerchief.*)

LAWRENCE: (*Pacing left and right.*) I don't know what it is. Lay awake through the night, staring at beams, counting configurations (*Wipes his brow with handkerchief.*), patterns on the ceiling—seeing things in the dark—

UNCLE DEL: (*Wringing out skin.*) What kind of things?

LAWRENCE: (*Continues pacing.*) I don't know—faces, maybe. Beings, bats. Why is it, ordinary people, any old body in the world—two people who don't even want kids, who just want to, you know, have fun— Why is it those people get pregnant like rabbits and abandon their offspring in dumpsters while we—us—mature, honest citizens of the community who actually want to have a child, end up—

UNCLE DEL: Have you tried it, doggy-style?

(LAWRENCE *stops in his tracks as* UNCLE DEL *crosses upstage with dripping skin and hangs it to dry on a clothesline.*)

LAWRENCE: (*After pause.*) Yes, actually. We have. We've experimented with several different positions—

UNCLE DEL: (*Hanging up skin.*) To no avail?

LAWRENCE: (*Starts pacing again.*) Exactly.

(DEL *pulls on the clothesline, which is on a pulley. Other skins appear from offstage.* DEL *turns and crosses downstage to the stool again. He sits on the stool, picks up a glass full of bull's blood, and drinks.*)

UNCLE DEL: Her mounting you, backwards?

LAWRENCE: (*Stops.*) Excuse me?

UNCLE DEL: Her—you know—astride you, with her ass to your head. You know—you on your back.

LAWRENCE: (*Pacing again.*) Oh, yes. Of course.

UNCLE DEL: Standing?

LAWRENCE: What?

UNCLE DEL: Both of you standing up. Vertical penetration.

LAWRENCE: Yes.

UNCLE DEL: Squatting?

LAWRENCE: Yes!

UNCLE DEL: Sitting?

LAWRENCE: (*Pacing.*) Yes!

UNCLE DEL: Underwater?

LAWRENCE: Yes!

UNCLE DEL: Mud?

LAWRENCE: (*Stops.*) What?

UNCLE DEL: In the mud?

LAWRENCE: Like pigs or something?

UNCLE DEL: Rutting, we used to call it. In the old days. Back in the good old days.

LAWRENCE: I don't know. (*Begins pacing again.*) I don't want to hear about this.

(DEL *pulls out a set of three knucklebones and rolls them on the floor in front of his stool. He drinks and reads the bones. Makes notes in a ledger he pulls out from under the stool.*)

UNCLE DEL: (*Rolling bones.*) You don't remember or—

LAWRENCE: (*Pacing.*) I don't remember, no. Yes, that's right. I don't remember.

UNCLE DEL: Seems like that would be something you wouldn't forget.

LAWRENCE: What?

UNCLE DEL: (*Making notes.*) Rutting in the mud. (*Rolling bones.*) Maybe you should drink some Memory Juice.

(*Offers his glass to* LAWRENCE, *who refuses.*)

LAWRENCE: (*Stops.*) Look— What're you doing?

UNCLE DEL: What? Oh, this? Rolling the Bones.

LAWRENCE: Rolling the Bones.

UNCLE DEL: Yes, futures, seeing ahead. Prescience. Same with the intestines on the line. (*Motions toward clothesline with dripping skins.*) They all tell a tale. Dreams. (*Toasts with glass.*) It's all written out somewhere.

(LAWRENCE *moves upstage toward the clothesline, stops in front of dripping skins, examines them.*)

LAWRENCE: These are somebody's intestines?

UNCLE DEL: (*Rolling bones.*) Somebody's sacrifice. They paid the price.

LAWRENCE: (*Touching a skin.*) Sacrificed?

UNCLE DEL: That's right. I believe they took the head off that one I just hung up.

LAWRENCE: What'd he do?

UNCLE DEL: Lied about his origins.

LAWRENCE: Origins. Is that all?

UNCLE DEL: That's enough.

LAWRENCE: (*Moves down toward* DEL.) So, do you have any advice for me?

UNCLE DEL: (*Continuing to throw bones.*) I do, as a matter of fact.

LAWRENCE: Good.

UNCLE DEL: This . . . seeming misfortune of yours, this childlessness—

LAWRENCE: Yes?

UNCLE DEL: It could turn out to be a blessing in disguise.

LAWRENCE: How do you mean?

UNCLE DEL: I have seen the horrible event projected. I have seen it painted in the bones.

LAWRENCE: What horrible event?

UNCLE DEL: Murder. I have seen the murder. There is no mistake.

LAWRENCE: Whose murder?

UNCLE DEL: Yours.

(LAWRENCE *immediately turns his back to* DEL *and drops to his knees, buries his face in his hands.* DEL *makes no reaction to this, keeps throwing bones.*)

UNCLE DEL: Any child born to you and your lovely queen, Jocasta, will turn out to be your killer and the husband of his mother.

LAWRENCE: (*Still on knees.*) No!!

UNCLE DEL: The bones never lie.

LAWRENCE: I don't want to hear about this.

UNCLE DEL: You're better off barren. Barren or dead.

(DEL *leaves bones onstage, picks up his stool, and exits. Lights shift down.* LAWRENCE *picks up bones, stares at them in his palm, stands, and moves up left. He is interrupted by* OEDIPUS, *entering from up center.*)

Scene 3

OEDIPUS: (*To* LAWRENCE.) What was this fear? Who first put it in you? Before my birth. Long before: Who put it there? Who first told you of my demon? Was it some treachery from far away? Across what sea? Who first told you about me? How could they have known?

(*A* terrible shrieking scream *from* JOCASTA. LAWRENCE *and* OEDIPUS *exit left. A cover is whipped off a steel cage by* HARRINGTON. JOCASTA *is trapped inside. The cage is rolled down right by actors who play* HARRINGTON *and* RANDOLPH. *They exit, leaving* JOCASTA *clinging to bars of cage, speaking to* LAWRENCE, *who is offstage, unseen.*)

Scene 4

JOCASTA: (*Up right, speaking from cage, holding bars.*) Larry? Why have you done this to me? This is not going to stop us, you know. It's not. A cage is not going to come between us—if that's what you think. Who told you this horror would originate in me? (*Pause while she listens. LAWRENCE appears between the dripping skins upstage with two bottles of wine. She doesn't see him.*) There's black wine in the basement. Stacks of it. Bring me two bottles and we'll dance. We'll sing. I'll take you back to those days when we couldn't stop touching. Remember those days? Larry? (LAWRENCE *reveals himself to her, approaches.*) Who told you to do this? Someone must have told you something. Who was it? What did they say? That I might cast some sort of curse on you? On us? On— Who was it, Larry? Tell me. You can talk to me. I won't give you away. There's black wine in the basement. Cobwebs and dust. Bring it up here, Larry, bring it.

(LAWRENCE *appears stage left with two bottles of wine. He stops and stares at* JOCASTA *in cage. He keeps approaching cage.*)

JOCASTA: (*To* LAWRENCE.) Oh, see, you've found it. I wasn't lying, was I. Bring it to me, Larry. That's right. Bring it here. (*Pause as* LAWRENCE *keeps slowly approaching cage.*) Was it something about the child? Is that it? A child that never was? Is that what they told you? Whoever— The child— You shouldn't listen to all that nonsense, Larry. Rumors—what does he know? Mumbo jumbo. Bones, blood, dreams, and guts dripping from clotheslines. I know his game. I've seen what he does. How he does it.

(LAWRENCE *manages to extract keys from his pocket. He unlocks the cage and lets* JOCASTA *out. She steps out of the cage and embraces him. He gently pushes her away and picks up a bottle of wine, then pours a glass for her that he draws from the bottle.*)

JOCASTA: (*Drinks, then . . .*) It was him, wasn't it? You shouldn't believe such wild superstitions. (*She slowly, seductively approaches him.* LAWRENCE *holds his ground.*) *Murder*— Is that what he told you? Murder and rape? That's not our fate. (*She pulls* LAWRENCE *toward her, embraces him, raises her skirt, and wraps a leg around his.* LAWRENCE *responds; they kiss passionately. She pulls back for a second.*)

JOCASTA: We'll see what comes of this.

(*They dance off upstage to tango music as lights go to half and* UNCLE DEL *comes onstage, embracing what looks to be old laundry or men's suits; he mimics the dance as* LAWRENCE *and* JOCASTA *go off. When he's alone,* DEL *signals musician to cut the music. Musician stops.*)

Scene 5

UNCLE DEL: (*Directly to audience, down center.*) What began it all, that's the question. I'll tell you what it is. You want to know? It's simple. But simple things are sometimes the hardest to hear, aren't they? Murder. Yes. That's what started this curse on our city. This disease. Plague. Epidemic. Murder. Plain and simple. Right here—years ago, just outside of town. Deserted highway. Desert. No wind to speak of. The bodies were all in pieces. (*He begins going around the stage distributing the old clothes as though they represented mangled corpses.*) The heads here. Arms and legs over there. They had to search for all the parts. The king's penis was missing. Imagine that! Some crow or coyote must have got it. Vandals, maybe. No matter. They put the bodies back together. Laid them out like a jigsaw puzzle. The king. That's what he was. Back when kings were kings. They say a band of bandits waylaid him—outnumbered and overwhelmed him. Others say a single man was the culprit. Ran him over with his own carriage. Scattered his parts and vanished. Now it's clear this murder has brought the trouble on us. An old defilement we may be sheltering. He's here among us now, this killer. Snickering at our misery. Slithering between our feet. Daring us to expose him—bring him into the light of day. Until we uncover this vermin we will continue to suffer our slow and painful disintegration. (*As he exits left.*) But who among you fears they'll find him in their own dark kitchen?

Scene 6

(*Highway 15, site of triple murder. Highway patrol officer* PATRICK HARRINGTON *is in full uniform, accompanied by forensic investigator* R. J. RANDOLPH *in an overcoat and blue latex gloves.* RANDOLPH *is squatting down over one of the ragged and bloody suits of clothes, picking up hair or thread with a tweezer and then dropping evidence into plastic bags while* HARRINGTON *strolls around through the corpses, taking notes and chewing on a candy bar.*)

HARRINGTON: Man oh man! Goddamn Mexicans! Can you believe it?

RANDOLPH: A little hasty to make that assumption right off the bat, Harrington.

HARRINGTON: Oh, really?

RANDOLPH: At this point it's wide-open. Could've been anyone.

HARRINGTON: Sure—maybe aliens or something, huh?

RANDOLPH: It appears to have been a spontaneous eruption of violence rather than an execution.

HARRINGTON: And what brings you to that, Mr. Scientist?

RANDOLPH: This first set of tire tracks. You see the way they're dug in there? Deep. Like he was making an escape, then changed his mind.

(HARRINGTON *crosses to imaginary tracks and examines them.*)

HARRINGTON: Yeah, well, he saw they weren't completely dead, so he came back to finish 'em off.

RANDOLPH: Had to have been out of rage, though. There is little indication of gang warfare or dope of any kind.

HARRINGTON: Rage? How do you know what this guy was feeling? It's just a set of damn tire tracks.

RANDOLPH: How many times do you think these bodies were run over?

HARRINGTON: A bunch. How should I know?

RANDOLPH: Seventeen times. He didn't just want them dead, he wanted them annihilated.

HARRINGTON: Seventeen times! Well, that fits with execution, doesn't it?

RANDOLPH: A little over the top, don't you think? I'm seeing another picture here.

HARRINGTON: You know what gets my hair up about all you forensic dudes?

RANDOLPH: (*Busy with the investigation.*) What's that, Harrington?

HARRINGTON: You think you know everything.

RANDOLPH: Is that right?

HARRINGTON: Yeah. You patchwork all this shit together and suddenly you've got a crystal ball or something.

RANDOLPH: Something like that.

HARRINGTON: Tire tracks, bones, teeth, pieces of cloth.

RANDOLPH: They all tell a story.

HARRINGTON: What story's that?

RANDOLPH: The story of what happened. What took place. Moments in the past, ticking away, one click at a time. It's incredible, isn't it?

HARRINGTON: Incredible.

RANDOLPH: Mounting up. Building to a climax. An eruption of fury. It all makes sense, suddenly.

HARRINGTON: None of it makes any sense! Are you kidding? This is just—this is just plain old slaughter, butchery. Like the old days.

RANDOLPH: Old days?

HARRINGTON: Disemboweling, hearts torn out, drawn and quartered, heads rolling. Blood dripping down the altar steps.

RANDOLPH: Oh, ancient, then?

HARRINGTON: Ancient, yes, but—

RANDOLPH: Everything has a history, doesn't it? I mean, this stuff didn't come out of thin air.

HARRINGTON: No, but I mean—there's a difference.

RANDOLPH: What's different?

HARRINGTON: You claim to see something. You claim to know exactly how it all happened. As though you were looking at a slow-motion movie.

RANDOLPH: (*Standing, moving to imaginary footprints.*) Look, come and take a look at these footprints here. (HARRINGTON *follows him.*) You see that pair of prints? That pair with the heavy tread, especially on the left foot?

HARRINGTON: What about it?

RANDOLPH: That's the killer, right there.

HARRINGTON: How do you know that?

RANDOLPH: He's standing alone by the side of the road. Outside the vehicle. Outside the story. Standing by himself. Maybe hitchhiking.

HARRINGTON: Hitchhiking?

RANDOLPH: Innocent.

HARRINGTON: What?

RANDOLPH: Completely innocent so far. He has no idea what's going to happen. Then a car comes along and everything changes. Very suddenly, everything changes.

HARRINGTON: Changes?

RANDOLPH: Car stops. Driver gets out and approaches the hitchhiker. Two guys are left in the backseat. Car's still idling. The driver's door is open.

HARRINGTON: Why does the driver get out of the car?

RANDOLPH: That, we don't know.

HARRINGTON: Ah.

RANDOLPH: The driver insults him. Hitchhiker takes offense.

HARRINGTON: What was the insult?

RANDOLPH: That's where it all begins. (*Points to the ground.*) Right there. A scuffle.

HARRINGTON: (*Looking at the ground.*) That's a scuffle?

RANDOLPH: Murder. Rage. Then a second guy comes from the car. Look. Right here. (HARRINGTON *follows close as* RANDOLPH *retraces the events on the floor.*) He comes much quicker. Probably pulls a weapon. Then a third man. Langos himself, maybe. And this is where the hitchhiker panics.

HARRINGTON: Panics? He's the killer.

RANDOLPH: Exactly. It's all about panic.

HARRINGTON: What happens now?

RANDOLPH: Hitchhiker runs to the car with two of them chasing him. Maybe the engine is still running. Maybe Langos left the door open. Maybe the car radio is playing, Sam Cooke, Percy Sledge. The guy jumps in the open door and guns the massive engine. First guy he runs over is Langos. Langos, just standing there thinking it's all being taken care of. The Boss. The Kingpin. He may even be going for a Cuban cigar at this point. (RANDOLPH *picks up a squashed butt of a cigar and hands it to* HARRINGTON.) Thinking about his beautiful long-legged girlfriend. The white beach of Cancún.

HARRINGTON: Oh, come on.

RANDOLPH: Before he can go for his lighter, the hitchhiker runs him over. Right here. Just levels him. Langos goes down and the guy heads for the highway with the other two chasing him. He sees them in the rearview mirror, pops it into reverse, and backs over the two wiseguys.

HARRINGTON: So they're all dead now?

RANDOLPH: Half dead. Takes a lot to kill someone with a car in one lick, unless you're lucky. Langos is twisting around in the sand still with his girlfriend in mind. Maybe he calls out her name. (*Shouting.*) "Dolores!"

HARRINGTON: Dolores?

RANDOLPH: The other two are screaming and firing at the car. Cursing. Metal's popping. Shattered glass. Burning rubber. The guy plows into Langos again, roars right over the top of him. This time he's dead. The image of his beautiful black-haired girlfriend floats out across the highway and dissolves into the hot wind. Still, shots are ringing out and angry shouts from the two lackeys. The guy finishes them off. Methodically. He crushes them over and over again. Back and forth with the car, vengeful fury. There is no mercy in this man.

HARRINGTON: Who the hell is he?

RANDOLPH: Yes! Exactly. That's the whole question, isn't it, Harrington? Who is he?

(*In blackout,* HARRINGTON *and* RANDOLPH *exit. Lights up on . . .*)

Scene 7

(MANIAC OF THE OUTSKIRTS *crosses extreme downstage,*
then hitchhikes with right arm. He's facing stage left, speaks
to imaginary audience; sometimes to his own shadow, cast
on wall.)

MANIAC: You! You think it's possible to hide from me? Have
you got any vague notion who I am? Who I'm intended
to be? I thought not. Just another vagabond, I suppose. Invisible. Lost through the cracks. Little do you
realize— Have you any idea whatsoever who you're
dealing with? Where I come from? My powerful lin-
eage? My father— My father, for instance, had one of
the largest, most expansive Chevy dealerships in the
entire county of San Bernardino! *That* surprises you,
doesn't it? Takes you back some. The whole stinking
county! Sold more Chevys than ten men over those
decades. Those early decades when Chevy was king!
Just hitting its stride, with the fins and all. Chrome! You
never saw chrome like that! Bumpers flashing, hood
ornaments parading, back when steel ruled the uni-

verse! Detroit in all its glory! A shining beacon. Passed you by like dust in the rearview mirror, didn't it! Dust! Well, just remember one thing: I am *not* anonymous. I am not going to just crumble away into oblivion. I will live forever! Don't forget that. Don't forget that.

Scene 8

(OTTO *emerges from upstage in his wheelchair, which is being pushed by his wife,* JOCELYN. *She also carries a small foldout breakfast table.* OTTO *is reading a police report from a newspaper as they continue. They stop downstage center.* JOCELYN *unfolds the table.* OTTO *continues reading as she listens.*)

OTTO: "California highway patrol officer Patrick Harrington reported finding three badly disfigured corpses in the desert off the shoulder of Highway 15 at approximately six p.m. Sunday, on the outskirts of Barstow. One of them without a face!"

JOCELYN: (*Exiting down right.*) Dusk. It's so pretty out there at dusk.

OTTO: (*Continues reading in his wheelchair.*) "The bodies seemed to have been deliberately and repeatedly run over by a heavy vehicle, leaving the rib cages crushed and flattened, the knees smashed, and the heads completely obliterated beyond recognition. Intestines and brains were scattered across the blacktop. Crows and buzzards interfered with the investigation."

JOCELYN: Lord have mercy! (*Coming back on with breakfast place settings from down left.*)

OTTO: (*Reading.*) "The vehicle apparently used in the gruesome murders was located early Monday morning in the parking lot of a Cucamonga liquor store."

JOCELYN: The Oasis? I always thought that was a bad location for a liquor store.

OTTO: (*Reading.*) "A steel-gray Bentley Phantom registered to one Angel Langos, the notorious Las Vegas casino mobster and drug lord."

JOCELYN: (*Setting the table.*) Here we go again.

OTTO: (*Reading.*) "Although authorities have not officially released the report, it is believed that the bodies were in fact Mr. Langos, his chauffeur, and his bodyguard, Vincent 'The Hawk' Mangolin. Evidence retrieved from the front and rear bumpers of the Bentley *strongly* indicates that the DNA blood type and hair samples belonged to the three victims aforementioned."

JOCELYN: I told you I never wanted to live this close to the border.

OTTO: We're nowhere near Mexico.

JOCELYN: Near enough.

OTTO: It's all in your mind, Jocelyn. Mexico is far, far away. It's all in your mind.

JOCELYN: How do you want your eggs?

OTTO: Poached, please. As usual. (JOCELYN *exits toward down right again.*) You know that way when you spin them?

JOCELYN: (*Stops, turns to* OTTO.) Spin?

OTTO: Where you whirl the boiling water so they look like little pudgy white jellyfish in a vortex. I like them like that.

JOCELYN: I'll do my best. (*Turns to go.*) Vortex?

OTTO: You've done them like that before, you know.

JOCELYN: (*As she exits.*) Like I say, I'll give it a whirl.

(LANGOS *enters upstage, smoking a cigar in the doorway.*)

OTTO: (*Pause as he puzzles over the article again;* JOCELYN *still off.*) You wanna know what I think? I think this guy must've been in competition with Langos. The killer. Another damn mobster or something. Casinos, maybe. Prostitution. Trafficking of some kind. Something ugly's going on.

(JOCELYN *reenters slowly, carrying two cups of coffee, sets them down on the table.*)

JOCELYN: (*Trying not to spill.*) Makes sense.

OTTO: They're out there making deals in the desert.

JOCELYN: Hanky-panky.

OTTO: Out where nobody can observe them. Twentynine Palms or somewhere.

JOCELYN: Ludlow.

OTTO: Yeah, maybe, Ludlow. Maybe Daggett. You wanna go out there, the scene of the crime?

JOCELYN: Are you kidding?

OTTO: Why not? A little adventure. Nobody's out there now. They're long gone.

JOCELYN: I'm not getting involved.

OTTO: We might find out something. A clue. Something overlooked.

JOCELYN: My "adventure days" are over.

OTTO: Yeah—maybe.

JOCELYN: When did all this happen, anyway?

OTTO: Sunday.

JOCELYN: That's when they found the bodies?

OTTO: Right.

JOCELYN: But it could've happened earlier. The killings.

OTTO: I suppose.

JOCELYN: A day or two.

OTTO: I don't know. (*Pause.*) What are you getting at?

JOCELYN: Whoever this guy was, he must've had a big, big grudge.

OTTO: It reminds me of something, once— (*Pause.*)

JOCELYN: What?

OTTO: A memory—something. I just got this little flash. A glimmer—

JOCELYN: Glimmer?

OTTO: Yeah, a little fragment. Like when you were a kid. I don't know. Just a glimpse, maybe.

JOCELYN: Of what?

OTTO: Guts on the highway.

JOCELYN: Jesus, Otto.

(*Black smoke is coming from down left.*)

OTTO: Toast is burning.

(JOCELYN *exits quickly down left,* OTTO *stays. Lights to black.*)

Scene 9

(LAWRENCE *enters in suit from up center. He crosses down center to audience.* OTTO *is gone.*)

LAWRENCE: (*Directly to audience.*) My father never touched the ground. He was always carried by slaves from place to place. Straddling their necks, his legs tucked inside their powerful arms. Gleaming sweat. They never stopped moving when they had to transport him a distance. They passed him from man to man as they ran across the mountains. When they finally set him down, his bare feet brushed silken tapestries, not the earth. Leopards woven in Persian yarn. Green parrots flapping wild through desert palms. He slept in hammocks of sweet grass, swinging softly in the shade of the honey locust. My father was never allowed to be kissed by the sun. The sun was not the most powerful force in the heavens at that time. My father was.

(JOCASTA *enters and crosses the back of the stage, pregnant. She comes forward and brushes past him as she exits down left. He follows.*)

(*Cross-fade to* OEDIUPUS, *extreme upstage in single spotlight.*)

Scene 10

OEDIPUS: (*Very still. Speaks to audience. Same costume; same eyes gouged out, dripping blood.*) You can't know how my heart did dances when I got the news. At last there was a reason . . . for our calamity. We knew we were looking for a killer now. The air reeked from corpses piling up. The sky black with vultures. Dogs skulked around in bony packs dragging ragged legs and arms. Fights broke out over every tiny morsel. Eyeballs. Noses. Ears. Shanks of hair and lips. The haunted faces of naked citizens seeing their death before them. Picking through scraps and burning heaps of carnage. Smoke streaked the sun. Now, at least, we knew. We had the answer. A deathly thing, beyond cure. The murderer at large in our very midst. This human beast had brought the disease upon us. Murder of a former king, way before my time. Slaughtered on the common highway by some vagabond maniac of the outskirts. We had only now to root him out. Blood for blood. He was our one salvation.

Scene 11

MANIAC: (*Alone, speaking to the wall and the audience.*) So of course, of course you charge me with some murder you can't put your finger on! Some wholesale slaughter by the side of the road. Some act of dementia. Must be on account of me right? Homeless! That's how you piece this thing together—this detective act. Perfect scene of the crime. Me! An innocent bystander trying to hitch a ride. That's all. Passing through. Innocent! Anonymous. Totally innocent! Now you even put up signs by the side of the road. "Don't pick up hitchhikers! Hitchhikers could be fleeing felons!" Rapists! Sodomists! Perverts! Vermin of the lowest caste. There was a time when hitchhiking was a respected art. Back in the days of the Depression. The good ol' days. Dust Bowl. Soup lines. People were generous back then. They'd give you handouts. A place to stay. A hunk of bread. Now what? Paranoia! Suspicion! Accusations of the most heinous kind.

Scene 12

(ANNALEE *enters, slowly pushing her father,* OTTO, *in the wheelchair, leisurely strolling around the stage.*)

OTTO: (*In his wheelchair.*) How come— Why is it you never come visit me anymore, Annalee?

ANNALEE: I never know where to find you, Dad.

OTTO: I'm around. I'm always around.

ANNALEE: Around where?

OTTO: Here. There. Everywhere.

ANNALEE: You've got no phone. No texting, no e-mail, no Facebook, Twitter. Nothing. Absolutely nothing.

OTTO: You found me easy enough.

ANNALEE: Yeah, yeah, I did. Just followed your trail of blood.

OTTO: (*Long pause.*) How you been?

ANNALEE: Can't complain.

OTTO: How's that guy? That idiot you had the kid with?

ANNALEE: Jimmy.

OTTO: That's his name? Jimmy?

ANNALEE: That's the kid's name.

OTTO: Oh.

ANNALEE: The father's name is James.

OTTO: James and Jimmy.

ANNALEE: Yeah.

OTTO: Pretty close.

ANNALEE: But I never call James, Jimmy.

OTTO: Oh, why's that?

ANNALEE: I don't want to confuse them.

OTTO: Right.

ANNALEE: He doesn't even deserve a name. (*Pause.*) He's in prison.

OTTO: Why's that?

ANNALEE: He killed somebody.

OTTO: Oh. Right. Who'd he kill this time?

ANNALEE: Our babysitter. He says he doesn't remember.

OTTO: No. He never does.

ANNALEE: Boned her to death.

OTTO: Figures.

ANNALEE: Left a big mess all over the windows.

OTTO: Right.

ANNALEE: Looks like some giant insect hit the glass.

OTTO: Nasty.

ANNALEE: Me and little Jimmy had to get out of there.

OTTO: Sure.

ANNALEE: It was too creepy.

OTTO: Of course.

ANNALEE: I tried mopping it up, but it was very sticky.

(*Long pause.*)

OTTO: (*Still being pushed by* ANNALEE.) Did you ever have this dream—this nightmare where you thought you might have killed someone?

ANNALEE: (*Stops suddenly.*) No!

(*She runs upstage, leaving* OTTO *in the wheelchair; stops again with her back to him.*)

OTTO: What's the matter now?

ANNALEE: (*Stays.*) I don't know.

OTTO: I've had that nightmare myself. I'm not sure who the victim was. I'm not even sure why.

ANNALEE: (*Stays.*) Don't!

OTTO: What?

ANNALEE: (*Stays.*) No more!

OTTO: No more what? I'm your father.

ANNALEE: (*Turning suddenly back to* OTTO.) I know that!

OTTO: I'll always be your father.

ANNALEE: (*Returns to* OTTO *and starts pushing him again.*) I know.

OTTO: You're awfully touchy lately. Things okay back home?

ANNALEE: NO! No, things are *not* okay back home. I just told you. Don't you listen?

OTTO: I always listen.

ANNALEE: My kid's marked for life.

OTTO: Marked?

ANNALEE: Scarred. Branded.

OTTO: (*They stop abruptly.*) Oh. His ankle?

(*BLACKOUT.*)

Scene 13

(*Lights up on* UNCLE DEL, *seated center stage in front of steaming bucket. He's stirring it with a long stick.*)

UNCLE DEL: (*To audience as he stirs bucket.*) You give advice. They ask for it, you give it. Simple. I don't mind. Really. I don't mind at all. I don't expect anything out of it. Certainly not monetary compensation. It's all free. All of it. Why they keep coming to me is a mystery, tell the truth. In droves sometimes, they come. Lines. Limping. Begging on their hands and knees for the truth. As though it were the rarest thing on earth. As though it were hidden somehow. Sequestered away. Smacks them night and day directly in the face—yet they come to me, asking for it. Why? As though belief had to come through someone else. Somewhere outside themselves. I tell them no different than what they already suspect. Things are hopeless. Futile. Obliteration. Annihilation. They cringe when they hear it, but all the while they've known. All the while they've felt it creep in their bones. That's the part that baffles me. They know. They already know.

Scene 14

(Cross-fade light to ANNALEE *and her father,* OTTO, *sitting side by side on bench, facing the audience, her arm tucked into his elbow.)*

OTTO: Jimmy still in prison?

ANNALEE: James!

OTTO: Right. James. Still in jail?

(She nods, facing the audience.)

OTTO: So he *did* kill the babysitter after all?

ANNALEE: He did.

OTTO: They convicted him?

ANNALEE: They did.

OTTO: The evidence must have been overwhelming.

ANNALEE: It was.

OTTO: Beyond a shadow of a doubt.

ANNALEE: Uh-huh.

OTTO: Open-and-shut case.

ANNALEE: Something they found in the mess.

OTTO: On the window, you mean?

ANNALEE: On the glass—yeah.

OTTO: What was it? Did they say?

ANNALEE: They say . . . they say they found a tinge of rage in the blood.

OTTO: Rage?

(*She nods.*)

OTTO: His blood or hers?

ANNALEE: Rage in his. Terror in hers.

OTTO: So they must've been mixed, then? The blood.

ANNALEE: Musta been.

OTTO: He must have been somehow cut in the killing. To have shed blood, I mean.

ANNALEE: Musta been.

OTTO: How was that? Did he use a weapon?

ANNALEE: Dunno. Maybe her earrings.

OTTO: Earrings?

ANNALEE: She wore these big star-shaped earrings. They hung down. Like knives.

OTTO: Sharp?

ANNALEE: I guess.

OTTO: Must've cut his hands, then? The earrings—when he was—

ANNALEE: His face, too. There were marks on his face.

OTTO: You saw marks on his face?

(*She nods.*)

ANNALEE: Looked as though he'd been clawed by an animal.

OTTO: (*After pause.*) How'd they tell it was rage, by the blood?

ANNALEE: Color, I guess. They have all kinds of ways of testing these days.

OTTO: Color?

ANNALEE: Pinkish, they said.

OTTO: And hers? The terror?

ANNALEE: Deep red.

Scene 15

LANGOS: (*Entering from upstage to extreme downstage center—direct to audience.*) It's not as though I'd forgotten him entirely, put him out of my mind. That's impossible, isn't it? The brain remembers everything—the human brain. These "tellers of tales" never know what goes on inside a man's feelings. They turn things to suit their own needs. Plot twists, story—inventions to make the listener think he's onto something while all the while intestines are roiling, blood is shooting itself into the heart. (*Rest.*) I had him always in my mind, hanging there helpless upside down from the bough of an olive tree. I never heard him scream or whimper—just watched him twisting there in the salty air with no one around but me. I often wondered what became of him. I did. Torn apart by wolves, birds of prey. Found and cut down by some kind soul. Tortured, maybe, by she-goat chimeras. I didn't know. So the idea came to me to visit the very same place on my way back to my ancient home. The very same tree. I reached the base of the mountain where I'd left him, but there was nothing but a man on the road, a common hitchhiker. Alone. He walked right out in front of the car, waving his arms and forcing us to stop. He had no shirt and one of his feet seemed much bigger than the other one. His eyes—I'll never forget—his eyes were wild and it seemed he'd never seen a human being before. He couldn't speak. His eyes were weeping and he couldn't speak.

(*Exits with light shift.*)

Scene 16

(*Lights up to discover* TRAVELER — *played by same actor as* UNCLE DEL — *an old man seated cross-legged center stage — head down, eyes on the ground in front of him, blind. He holds a cane out, sketching circles.* ANNALEE *enters at a run with infant wrapped in a yellow blanket. She stops when she sees* TRAVELER, *bounces baby softly on her hip, hums an unidentifiable tune. Pause.*)

ANNALEE: Sir? Sir, could I speak to you for a second?

TRAVELER: (*Slowly raising his head.*) You are.

ANNALEE: I— I didn't expect to find anyone up here, so far from . . . I mean, what is it you do way out here? Are you just by yourself?

TRAVELER: I have my — goats and sheep.

ANNALEE: Oh, I see. You *live* out here, then?

TRAVELER: I have my trailer.

ANNALEE: Right. And you—do you go to town much?

TRAVELER: Never.

ANNALEE: Oh. Good. I mean, I was—do you think you could do me a big favor?

TRAVELER: What?

ANNALEE: My child, my son. He's—he's seen something terrible that . . . I think it's going to take him awhile to get over it. I mean, I'm not sure he'll ever get over this, but I need to leave him for a while. Do you understand?

TRAVELER: No.

ANNALEE: I need to leave him and come back.

TRAVELER: When?

ANNALEE: Well . . .

TRAVELER: You want to abandon him, is that it?

ANNALEE: No!

TRAVELER: You want to leave him in a dumpster, but there's no dumpster up here, is there? No convenient trash cans.

ANNALEE: No! That's not—I do *not* want to abandon him! That's not what I want to do.

TRAVELER: But that's what you're going to do.

ANNALEE: No! (*Turns away from him.*)

TRAVELER: Can I sell him?

ANNALEE: Absolutely not!

TRAVELER: Give him away?

ANNALEE: Never mind!

TRAVELER: Why do you pretend to care what happens to him?

(*She stops, turns.*)

ANNALEE: There's no pretending. I'm not pretending! I'm his mother.

TRAVELER: Then what is it?

ANNALEE: I'm looking for a home for him!

TRAVELER: *You're* his only home.

ANNALEE: Look, mister, I'm sorry. I thought—

TRAVELER: It's too late to be sorry for anything. It's always too late.

ANNALEE: (*Stares at him.*) Are you blind?

TRAVELER: All I see is wreckage.

ANNALEE: I'm —

TRAVELER: What is it *he* saw? The boy. Something horrible, you say?

ANNALEE: Yes.

TRAVELER: Something so horrible he can't live with it in his mind? He can't go on through life without being tormented by this vision?

ANNALEE: I think —

TRAVELER: What could be so horrible as that?

ANNALEE: His father.

TRAVELER: Ah.

ANNALEE: His father raped someone in front of him. While the baby was crawling around on the floor.

TRAVELER: Ah. And who was that?

ANNALEE: What?

TRAVELER: That his father raped.

ANNALEE: The babysitter.

TRAVELER: Ah. That is horrible.

ANNALEE: I think he might have killed her.

TRAVELER: Really?

ANNALEE: He's going to jail.

TRAVELER: For killing or rape?

ANNALEE: Both, I think.

TRAVELER: And you think the child is going to carry that experience with him for the rest of his life?

ANNALEE: I don't know.

TRAVELER: What if he forgets the whole thing?

ANNALEE: How could he?

TRAVELER: He's very young yet. There's no way you can know, is there?

ANNALEE: No. I guess not, but—

TRAVELER: So what good is it going to do if you abandon him here?

ANNALEE: I'm not abandoning him, goddamnit!!

TRAVELER: You're trying to kill him? Is that it?

ANNALEE: Oh, fuck you!

(*She storms off. He stops her with his voice.*)

TRAVELER: *I'll* kill him for you. (*She stops cold, her back to him.*) How much have you got?

ANNALEE: (*Turning slowly toward him.*) Not much.

TRAVELER: (*Laughs.*) A nickel?

ANNALEE: Don't laugh at me.

TRAVELER: You want no trace left of him, I suppose? Not even a toenail.

ANNALEE: I can't.

TRAVELER: What?

ANNALEE: I can't bear him growing up with this nightmare.

TRAVELER: You don't know.

ANNALEE: What?

TRAVELER: You don't know what's going to happen. He may become a legendary man. A hero. Honored and revered.

ANNALEE: No.

TRAVELER: You don't know. He could become anything.

ANNALEE: I—

TRAVELER: Maybe it's just *you* who can't take it.

ANNALEE: What?

TRAVELER: The pictures in your mind. The imagery.

ANNALEE: I've got no pictures.

TRAVELER: Your husband bumping the babysitter. Maybe it's only you. Killing your baby won't fix that.

ANNALEE: Look, mister—

TRAVELER: I'll do it for twenty bucks.

ANNALEE: What!

TRAVELER: Ten dollars, then.

ANNALEE: Are you out of your mind?

TRAVELER: Five. That's as low as I go.

(ANNALEE *storms off.*)

ANNALEE: You goat fucker!

TRAVELER: Where are you going?

ANNALEE: I left my purse in the car! (*She exits.*)

TRAVELER: (*To himself.*) There's no rush.

(*Lights shift.* TRAVELER *exits in dark.*)

Scene 17

(OEDIPUS *comes charging onto extreme down center. Fero-cious—direct to audience. His eyes are the same red gashes.* JOCASTA *follows him and watches.*)

OEDIPUS: (*Direct to audience.*) Until now I was a stranger to this tale. A stranger to the crime. How could this be? All this time lurking among us like the slinking dogs, from corpse to corpse. Any common day I could have brushed up against him in the marketplace. Seen him eye to eye. Not knowing. Even now he could have the audacity to be sitting right here amongst us. Inwardly sneering in our midst. Licking his chops like the green-eyed hyena. Let me tell you that if anyone here has the slightest suspicion who might have been the killer—or worse, may be harboring this demon—let him come forward and surrender with the promise that no further tribulation will come to him. Banishment will occur in utter safety. Know also that I solemnly forbid anyone to receive this man or speak to him, no matter who he pretends to be in the community. He must be driven from every house, every nesting place; shunned as you've shunned the plague bearers akin to you. I pray that this man's life be consumed in evil and wretchedness. And I vouch that this curse applies no less to me, should it turn out that somehow he has conned his way into my company, sharing my family and hearth. I now take the son's part in this revenge as though the king were my own blood father. I will see this thing through to the naked end.

(JOCASTA *and* OEDIPUS *exit.*)

Scene 18

(Lights on ANNALEE *by herself, leaning against wall. She seems to speak to the audience and herself at the same time.)*

ANNALEE: Sometimes I see me and Dad like an old black-and-white movie flickering outside my head. Way outside. We're walking. Straight ahead. Me leading. He's poking his crooked stick against stones and brush. As though searching for something—something he lost. I don't know where we are. Some open place. Not here. His eyes are gone. Black holes. He's very old and thin. Bent, like his walking stick. I know what he's looking for. Even without his eyes, I can tell.

Scene 19

(HARRINGTON *and* RANDOLPH *continue to gather evidence: lay out yellow tape, make measurements, etc.*)

RANDOLPH: Did you bring the water? Where's the water?

HARRINGTON: What water?

RANDOLPH: (*Pause, stares at him.*) The water. H_2O. Something wet.

HARRINGTON: We went through the bottled stuff.

RANDOLPH: How long have we been out here?

HARRINGTON: Awhile.

RANDOLPH: And we've already been through the bottled stuff?

HARRINGTON: Pretty much.

RANDOLPH: And you didn't bring any additional water? No jug or anything?

HARRINGTON: Well, I brought the bottled water, like I said.

RANDOLPH: Do you realize where we are?

HARRINGTON: Yeah, of course I realize where we are.

RANDOLPH: We're in the middle of the Mojave.

HARRINGTON: I know that. Don't you worry about that. I know where we are.

RANDOLPH: And you didn't bring any water? I mean, additional water?

HARRINGTON: I can run down to Ludlow in the squad car and get some. It's not that far.

RANDOLPH: Ludlow?

HARRINGTON: Yeah, the Quick Stop.

RANDOLPH: The Quick Stop at Ludlow?

HARRINGTON: Yeah. They got water.

RANDOLPH: Expensive by the bottle.

HARRINGTON: We can get it out of the hose, then.

RANDOLPH: They've got a hose there? In Ludlow?

HARRINGTON: They always have a hose. All those Quick Stops. Right next to the tire-pressure thing.

RANDOLPH: I'm not drinking water out of a hose. Tastes like rubber. Sitting there, coiled in the sun.

HARRINGTON: Then I'll buy some more bottled water. I got change. I hate paying for water. (*Fishes for change in his pockets.*)

RANDOLPH: Okay.

HARRINGTON: I'll get the car, then. You coming?

RANDOLPH: Of course I'm coming. I'm not sitting out here all alone under the broiling sun while you drive around in an air-conditioned squad car.

HARRINGTON: I'll be right back.

RANDOLPH: I'm coming with you. What if you get in a car wreck?

HARRINGTON: There's no one out here . . .

(HARRINGTON *exits.* RANDOLPH *follows.*)

Scene 20

(OTTO *enters in the wheelchair, being pushed along by* JOC-
ELYN, *on the shoulder of Highway 15—scene of the crime.
They both stare down at the ground, looking for something
as they slowly stroll along.*)

JOCELYN: Are you sure this is the spot?

OTTO: You can see all the yellow chalk marks, can't you?
  Where they've measured the tire tracks, outlined the
  bodies? Distances. Places.

JOCELYN: I suppose.

OTTO: Well, this is it, then. Scene of the crime. Right in
  here. Has to be.

JOCELYN: I don't think we should be out here. What are we
  looking for exactly?

OTTO: I'm not quite sure. Something in the report—

JOCELYN: Report?

OTTO: The story in the newspaper.

JOCELYN: What about it?

OTTO: Something rang a bell. I don't know.

JOCELYN: A bell?

OTTO: Well, what was it you asked me before? I'm trying to remember what triggered this.

JOCELYN: When?

OTTO: Yesterday morning, when I was reading the article about the murders.

JOCELYN: Oh, I can't remember.

OTTO: About the day they discovered the bodies.

JOCELYN: What did I say?

OTTO: You asked me if it was Sunday. Right?

JOCELYN: Did I?

OTTO: Yes. And then you said it could've happened earlier.

JOCELYN: Oh.

OTTO: Earlier than Sunday.

JOCELYN: So?

OTTO: So that's what got me started.

JOCELYN: About what?

OTTO: The whole thing. As though it all could've happened long before this.

JOCELYN: Before Sunday, you mean?

OTTO: Long, long before Sunday.

JOCELYN: I don't get it. Why are you trying to make this so complicated, anyway? Three men were run over in a car by another man. Simple.

OTTO: I suppose if we knew how to read all these signs, we could put the whole thing back together.

JOCELYN: What signs?

OTTO: All these marks on the ground. Tires and footprints and marks. You know. Broken cactus.

JOCELYN: They must have taken photographs of everything already.

OTTO: I suppose.

JOCELYN: What a mess. Life is tough enough without running people over willy-nilly.

OTTO: Willy-nilly?

JOCELYN: Well, I mean—

OTTO: Willy-nilly?

JOCELYN: Just something from my past.

OTTO: Oh.

JOCELYN: I had a Welsh grandmother.

OTTO: "Willy-nilly" is Welsh? I didn't know that.

JOCELYN: Maybe not "willy-nilly" itself—the expression— but *she* was Welsh and she always used to say that. Well, let's not dwell on it.

OTTO: Wonder where *she* picked it up?

JOCELYN: Could've been her grandmother, I suppose.

OTTO: It's in the past.

JOCELYN: Or someone from the village, maybe.

OTTO: Village? It was *that* long ago?

JOCELYN: Her little village in Cardiff or wherever it was.

OTTO: Ah.

JOCELYN: "Willy-nilly," you know. As though to say—

OTTO: "Any old whichaway."

JOCELYN: Exactly.

OTTO: Higgledy-piggledy.

JOCELYN: That's enough!

OTTO: Topsy-turvy.

JOCELYN: Stop it! We should go back now. We're getting

really silly. We may lose our minds out here altogether, and there we'd be—

OTTO: Where?

JOCELYN: Out *here* on the highway. Who would stop for a couple of doddering old loonies like us?

OTTO: Yes. (*Sees something on the ground, far right.*) Wait!

JOCELYN: What? (*She stops; Otto points to something down right, at a distance.*)

OTTO: What's that?

JOCELYN: What?

OTTO: Don't you see it? Push me over there. Come on, come on.

JOCELYN: Take it easy.

(JOCELYN *pushes* OTTO *in the wheelchair over to where he's pointing.*)

OTTO: Stop. What's that?

(*She stops and looks down to where* OTTO'*s pointing.*)

JOCELYN: (*Trying to see the object.*) What?

OTTO: (*Pointing.*) That right there! Don't you see it?

JOCELYN: Oh.

OTTO: What's that?

(JOCELYN *crosses to a tiny piece of cloth sticking out of the floor, just the corner of something. She bends over and takes hold of it and begins pulling on it. Very slowly it comes out of the floor like a magic trick at the circus—the yellow blanket* ANNALEE *had wrapped the baby in.* JOCELYN *holds it up to the light, then lays it across* OTTO*'s lap.*)

(BLACKOUT.)

Scene 21

(ANNALEE *sings a cappella in the dark.*)

ANNALEE:

In tears I was born
In tears I will die
And life in between
Is the history of tears

Scene 22

(*Lights up on* LANGOS *as he comes strutting downstage, methodically macho, with a cell phone held tightly to his ear.*)

LANGOS: So now let me get this story straight. Apparently he didn't bleed to death from his ankle wound. Is that it? Some asshole saved him? Cut him down? Who? A hitchhiker? A lonely old man by the side of the road took pity on him? No, no, that can't be the case. No! Look, who exactly are you? Just an anonymous caller doing me a favor? Well, thank you very much. And what am I supposed to do with this information? Huh? What? Say that again. He's coming after me? (*Laughs.*) This punk kid is coming after me? You've got to be joking. Does he have any idea who he's dealing with—who I am? Look, what's he after? Money, is that it? How much does he want? Revenge? (*Laughs.*) Revenge? Who are you! Who does this kid think he is? My son! My son? No. No, no, you've got this whole thing screwed up! This is all a huge mistake! I have no son! No. Well, none to speak of. I mean, long ago, maybe. No, no, that's not true. That was in another life. That was— You're not his mother, are you? Is that it? No? Just a friend. An innocent friend. Of the family? No! There is no family! There never has been!

(*He hangs up and storms off upstage as* ANNALEE *storms on. The two of them pass each other with no sign of recognition.*)

Scene 23

ANNALEE: (*To audience, charging to down center.*)

Oh, tragedy, tragedy, tragedy, tragedy.
Piss on it.
Piss on Sophocles's head.
I'd rather be dead.
I would.
No lie.
You think I'm kidding?
Why waste my time?
Why waste yours?
What's it for?
Catharsis?
Purging?
Metaphor?
What's in it for us?
You and me.
All this harking shit up.
I ask you.
I ask myself.

I do, I do.

I'd rather not know.

Tell you the truth.

I go around and around and around and around about it.

I do, I do.

Am I better off?

No!

Are you?

I go around and around and around and around.

And I wind up here.

Right back here.

Just like you.

Exactly like you do.

What's in it for you and me?

A broken memory?

Scene 24

(*Lights up on* TRAVELER, *seated on bench up center.* OEDIPUS *enters.*)

OEDIPUS: So I see they've found you. Where were you hiding? Back with your goats again? Your burros.

TRAVELER: Someone informed me you've become keenly interested in the truth, suddenly.

OEDIPUS: We need to root this killer out. You've seen the state of things. They tell me nothing will get any better until we capture this maniac.

TRAVELER: Who's they?

OEDIPUS: The powers that be.

TRAVELER: I rarely come to town. I'm not up-to-date on things.

OEDIPUS: But you know— You can't help but know what's become of the country.

TRAVELER: Yes. Everything's gone to shit, hasn't it?

OEDIPUS: Hell in a handbasket.

TRAVELER: All the guts are now on the table.

OEDIPUS: So can you help us? We need to eliminate this killer before it's too late.

TRAVELER: You bear your fate and I'll bear mine.

OEDIPUS: You can't refuse this. They say you know who the killer is.

TRAVELER: The truth won't save you. The truth will only bring you down.

OEDIPUS: I'll be the judge of that!

TRAVELER: Not if I remain silent.

OEDIPUS: You can turn your back on your own country? Betray us all and ruin the state? If you can identify this criminal, it's your duty—

TRAVELER: Duty! My duty? If you could only see what I'm saving you from.

OEDIPUS: There are ways we can extract information, you know?

TRAVELER: Torture cannot touch me. You ought to know that by now.

OEDIPUS: I'll tell you what I think. I think it may be *you* we're searching for. The mastermind behind it all. Part of some creeping conspiracy.

TRAVELER: You're wildly splashing in your own madness now.

OEDIPUS: I'll have you arrested and brought before the courts and exposed as a fraud and an informer!

TRAVELER: All right! All right! (*Pause.*) You want to know? You want to know? Here's the thing you say you long for. The "truth" you say you want. Can you take it? Can you swallow it whole? *You yourself are the sickness behind this utter collapse.*

OEDIPUS: What? You can come stumbling in here, smelling of piss and goats, and make an accusation like this?

TRAVELER: You demanded it.

OEDIPUS: Say it again?

TRAVELER: It wasn't clear the first time?

OEDIPUS: Say it again! Don't play with me.

TRAVELER: *You* are the murderer you're looking for! *You* weave your own doom!

OEDIPUS: Bastard! (OEDIPUS *grabs him suddenly by the neck.*)

TRAVELER: (*Breaking free.*) I see you haven't lost your impulse!

OEDIPUS: (*Backing away.*) You drive me to it!

TRAVELER: You drive yourself.

OEDIPUS: Enough! You blind idiot!

TRAVELER: With both your naked healthy eyes, you are the one who cannot see.

OEDIPUS: What? What is it?! Tell me!

TRAVELER: The wretchedness of your own life. You can't see in whose house you live, nor with whom. Who are your mother and father? Can you answer me that? Who are your blood parents?

OEDIPUS: Who?

TRAVELER: The double lash of your parents' curse will whip you and send you reeling into exile.

OEDIPUS: What are you saying? (*Screaming.*) Who were my parents!! Who were they?

TRAVELER: This day will give you a father and break your heart.

Scene 25

(Lights up on ANNALEE, *to one side.)*

ANNALEE: I never thought of him as my brother. I don't now. They say he is. They've all told me. The world knows, but I don't. He's my father and always will be. I'll stick with him 'til his last days on earth. I'll hold his hand. I'll guide him. I'll be his eyes. I love him. I always will. I know what he's done—what they say about him. It doesn't matter. I love him still. It's a love that knows no bounds. No boundaries. He will live in me forever.

Scene 26

(*Lights up on* JOCASTA *and* OEDIPUS *facing each other. He is seated, facing a mirrored plate that* JOCASTA *holds up to his face.*)

JOCASTA: So, now, just tell me what you see.

OEDIPUS: (*Looking in mirror.*) I see— I see—

JOCASTA: What is it?

OEDIPUS: My self. I see myself.

JOCASTA: Do you see anything resembling a murderer?

OEDIPUS: No.

JOCASTA: A skulking dog?

OEDIPUS: No.

JOCASTA: A brother to his own son?

OEDIPUS: No.

JOCASTA: To his own daughter?

OEDIPUS: No.

JOCASTA: A killer of his father?

OEDIPUS: No.

JOCASTA: Husband to his mother?

OEDIPUS: No.

JOCASTA: Then what is this old fool who told you all these lies anything other than insane?

OEDIPUS: He was trusted—

JOCASTA: By who?

OEDIPUS: My parents, for one.

JOCASTA: Your parents?

OEDIPUS: Yes. They found him trustworthy.

JOCASTA: And who were these parents of yours?

OEDIPUS: They were in the distant city of—

JOCASTA: Where?

OEDIPUS: Far away. I can't remember.

JOCASTA: Where you grew up?

OEDIPUS: Yes.

JOCASTA: You can't remember?

OEDIPUS: No.

JOCASTA: Then how would this old blind man know if you yourself can't even remember? He was never there!

OEDIPUS: His story—

JOCASTA: What about it?

OEDIPUS: Something—

JOCASTA: All prophesies are hocus-pocus! Poppycock!

OEDIPUS: Something about—

JOCASTA: Tokenism! Cock-and-bull!

OEDIPUS: Something about the story—

JOCASTA: Treacherous! Mythomania!

OEDIPUS: Something about the story rang true!

(*Silence.* JOCASTA *puts the mirror in front of him again.*)

JOCASTA: What do you see, again?

OEDIPUS: I see—

JOCASTA: Yourself again.

OEDIPUS: I see . . . murder.

JOCASTA: No!

OEDIPUS: The most horrible—

JOCASTA: No!

OEDIPUS: Running, horses, cars on fire, burning flesh.

JOCASTA: No!

OEDIPUS: I see hordes of people. Screaming. Throwing stones.

JOCASTA: No!

OEDIPUS: I see people killing brothers. Skinning mothers. Rolling their fathers' heads down the street with sticks.

JOCASTA: He's put all this in your mind! That evil, evil man.

OEDIPUS: The street is lit with hatred. Their eyes are torches. Their tongues—

JOCASTA: Stop!

(*Pause.*)

OEDIPUS: I may have been the one.

JOCASTA: What?

OEDIPUS: The one they're looking for.

(*Silence.*)

JOCASTA: How is that possible?

OEDIPUS: Something about his story— I remember—

JOCASTA: What? You remember what?

OEDIPUS: A crossroads. The place.

JOCASTA: You were far, far away, you said. A boy. Another town. Your father—

OEDIPUS: My father may have been the one I slaughtered.

JOCASTA: That was another man! Another time!

OEDIPUS: What if it wasn't? What if I am the man they're looking for?

JOCASTA: He's trying to turn you. Make you doubt your real self.

OEDIPUS: Is it the truth we're after?

JOCASTA: Of course it is, but this old man is blind. How can he see the truth?

OEDIPUS: There is a memory. A face—

JOCASTA: Whose?

OEDIPUS: His face. Black with anger. His eyes. As though he wanted to crush me, grind me in the ground.

JOCASTA: It wasn't him. It was another man.

OEDIPUS: A king! They said he was a king!

JOCASTA: Of another land. Kings are a dime a dozen.

OEDIPUS: Not this one. He wanted me dead! Gone.

(JOCASTA *desperately holds the mirror in front of* OEDIPUS.)

JOCASTA: Tell me what you see!

OEDIPUS: Him! Slaughtered on the highway. Run over! Pulverized in rocks and gravel. It was me who ran him over! Me!!

JOCASTA: No!

OEDIPUS: There was no one else.

JOCASTA: If you grow to believe this lie, you will bring everything down upon you. There's no way you will survive the weight of it. It will splinter you into a million pieces like a giant fist you don't see coming. You will be smashed to bits.

OEDIPUS: There was no one there but me.

(OEDIPUS *and* JOCASTA *remain onstage with their backs turned toward audience. Light shifts slightly as* MANIAC *enters and speaks to* OEDIPUS.)

Scene 27

MANIAC: Now he'd trade spots with me, I'll bet—give anything to live in my pointless dilemma. Beg for a ride out of here. Wake up to find himself sleeping in dumpsters, covered in garbage and sheets of black plastic. Lavish in it. Now he'd gladly steal fruit from a vendor, socks from a clothesline. Go days rambling to only himself and stray dogs. What fleeting skin we wear. Every day shedding another layer until nothing's left but blood and muscle. The rain stings. Breeze is like razors across your back. Sun cooks me to the core. Fresh meat. I crawl in the shade of juniper. I crawl. Gladly.

(He exits upstage as light rises on JOCASTA *and* OEDIPUS.*)*

Scene 28

JOCASTA: (*Turning to* OEDIPUS.) Who told you the "truth" was such a good idea? You think they know the world? "The truth will set you free?" Ha! What a crock of shit that is. That's for sissies. That's for those who haven't got a clue. Flailing around in their own confusion. Swimming in a sea of failure and regret. A last resort. I'll tell you what the "truth" is for. It's for tearing us all apart. Suspicion! Treachery! That's what it brings down upon our heads. Sudden mistrust. There's not one out there that can tell you the unknowable. Not one. They're making it all up. Dreamers, and you've fallen into their web. (*Pause.*) Everyone knows the king was killed by a multitude of men, marauding strangers on the highway—not a single lone assassin. Certainly not his own flesh and blood. Everyone knows that. So how can some old blind man claim to have packed away this secret until today?

OEDIPUS: How strange. A shadow just crossed my mind.

JOCASTA: What shadow's that?

OEDIPUS: I saw the highway.

JOCASTA: Your mind is playing tricks.

OEDIPUS: What can I trust if not my mind?

JOCASTA: They're shaping things in you that don't exist.

OEDIPUS: Tell me how the king looked. How old was he?

JOCASTA: Tall. His hair streaked with white. His build was much like yours.

OEDIPUS: Was he alone or with a group?

JOCASTA: Why are you asking these things?

OEDIPUS: Was he alone!

JOCASTA: No. Yes. No.

OEDIPUS: Who told you how it happened? (*Pause.*) Who told you!

JOCASTA: He worked for the king.

OEDIPUS: Where is he now?

JOCASTA: I sent him away. I found him another job.

OEDIPUS: Why was that?

JOCASTA: I was afraid.

OEDIPUS: Of what?

JOCASTA: Someone.

OEDIPUS: Find him!

JOCASTA: I can't!

OEDIPUS: Find him now!

JOCASTA: What can he tell you that I haven't already?

OEDIPUS: He was there! He can tell me the truth!

(*Lights fade on their exit. Lights up on* LANGOS.)

Scene 29

LANGOS: When I was first told this tale, I thought I could dodge the implications. Run around it somehow. Avoid my fate the way you would a falling tree. You hear it cracking long before it hits the ground. I stole the baby from its mother. Tore it from her breast. I ran with it for miles until my chest was full of fire. There was no going back. No second thought. I bound its legs. Drove a stake through its left ankle and hung it upside down from an olive tree. I didn't hear it screaming. I saw birds. Clouds racing. But I didn't hear it scream. It was not a son to me. Just an enemy. A demon in disguise. Terror drove me to it. Only terror. It wasn't me.

(*Cross-fade on his exit.*)

Scene 30

(OEDIPUS *and* JOCASTA *facing* HARRINGTON, *with* RANDOLPH *sheepishly standing behind. They are at the very scene of the crime: Highway 15, near Barstow, California.*)

OEDIPUS: (*Pointing to* RANDOLPH.) Who's that man? Why is he here?

HARRINGTON: He was my partner, sir.

OEDIPUS: Partner?

HARRINGTON: On the case. Professional forensic investigator. Detective Ronald J. Randolph, sir. (HARRINGTON *nudges* RANDOLPH *out in front.* RANDOLPH *emerges, head down, extending a blue-gloved hand out to* OEDIPUS, *who refuses to shake it.* OEDIPUS *and* JOCASTA *stare at him coldly.*)

JOCASTA: He's just a lackey. (*To* HARRINGTON.) I told you to come alone.

HARRINGTON: Sorry, ma'am, but he has concrete evidence.

OEDIPUS: Of what?

HARRINGTON: The murder. DNA samples. Dirt. Spit. Hair. Blood. Even fingernail clippings.

OEDIPUS: Where are they? All these samples.

HARRINGTON: Take them out, Randolph. Show them.

(RANDOLPH *starts taking out all the various items, contained mostly in ziplock bags, including a crushed cigar butt, from his overcoat pockets and lines them all up in front of* OEDIPUS *on the floor.*)

JOCASTA: More conjury! Magic tricks. What is all this proof of?

HARRINGTON: Who was killed, ma'am. How they were killed. How many were present.

JOCASTA: How many?

HARRINGTON: Yes, ma'am.

OEDIPUS: Have you arrived at a number?

HARRINGTON: Four, sir.

OEDIPUS: Four?

JOCASTA: Were you there at the time the murder took place?

HARRINGTON: No, ma'am.

JOCASTA: Then how could you possibly know how many? Maybe there were more?

HARRINGTON: These things—

OEDIPUS: Do you recognize me? My face?

HARRINGTON: I know you're the king.

OEDIPUS: And how do you know that?

HARRINGTON: I was told.

JOCASTA: Hearsay.

OEDIPUS: Do you recognize me from the scene of the murder?

HARRINGTON: Like I said, I wasn't there.

OEDIPUS: (*To* RANDOLPH.) And how about you? Do you recognize me?

RANDOLPH: No, sir.

OEDIPUS: (*To* RANDOLPH.) Could you describe the murder to me? Do you have a picture of it in your head?

RANDOLPH: Yes, sir.

OEDIPUS: Let's hear it.

JOCASTA: Neither one of them was there!

OEDIPUS: I want to hear it.

JOCASTA: A fantasy!

RANDOLPH: Based on the evidence he was standing by the road—the highway.

OEDIPUS: Who was?

RANDOLPH: The killer.

OEDIPUS: Was he alone?

RANDOLPH: Yes, sir.

JOCASTA: And how do you know that?

RANDOLPH: Tracks, ma'am.

JOCASTA: His tracks?

RANDOLPH: Yes, ma'am. He was on foot. Very distinct.

JOCASTA: You said there were others! A group of bandits.

RANDOLPH: There was only one killer. One foot. The left one. Much bigger than the right.

(*All of their eyes, including* OEDIPUS's, *shift focus to his large left foot. Silence as they consider the repercussions.*)

JOCASTA: It's not proof! Just a mark in the sand! It could have been anyone. There were others!

OEDIPUS: It wasn't anyone. I've had this mark as long as I can remember.

JOCASTA: This talk is a waste of time. It's all speculation!

OEDIPUS: How can you say that when the clues of truth are in my hands?

JOCASTA: You are fatally wrong! May you never learn who you actually are.

OEDIPUS: How could I ever wish that I were someone else?

JOCASTA: Your misery will know no bounds! (JOCASTA *starts to leave, but then stops with her back to* OEDIPUS, *upstage.*)

JOCASTA: Learn to love death's ink-black shadow as much as you love the light of dawn.

(*She exits. Long silence.* HARRINGTON *gets spooked by it.*)

Scene 31

HARRINGTON: Where's she suddenly gone? (*Pause.*) Why this silence?

OEDIPUS: What would you fill it up with?

(RANDOLPH *starts nervously retrieving all the objects he's laid out and replacing them in his pockets. He drops the cigar butt in the process.*)

HARRINGTON: (*To* RANDOLPH.) What're you doing? We're not finished yet.

RANDOLPH: (*As he retrieves objects.*) My job is scientific, objective. Totally quantitative. I didn't come here for—

OEDIPUS: (*Picks cigar butt off the floor.*) What's this?

HARRINGTON: Part of the evidence, sir. We're pretty sure the victim was a cigar smoker.

OEDIPUS: (*Smelling butt.*) The victim?

HARRINGTON: Yes, sir.

OEDIPUS: Not the killer?

HARRINGTON: No, sir.

OEDIPUS: (*To* RANDOLPH.) You were telling the story. The story of the murder.

RANDOLPH: Well, based on our findings. We can't be sure.

OEDIPUS: (*Smelling cigar.*) This smell reminds me of something.

HARRINGTON: My father used to smoke a good cigar now and then.

OEDIPUS: Your father?

HARRINGTON: Yes, sir.

OEDIPUS: (*To* RANDOLPH.) Continue with the story, Detective.

RANDOLPH: Where was I?

OEDIPUS: He was standing by the side of the road. Hitchhiking, I believe.

RANDOLPH: Did I say that? Hitchhiking?

OEDIPUS: Yes, I believe you did.

RANDOLPH: (*To* HARRINGTON.) Did I say that?

HARRINGTON: No, I don't think so, sir. I don't think he said that—"hitchhiking."

OEDIPUS: Are you calling me a liar?

HARRINGTON: Well, no, of course not.

OEDIPUS: (*To* RANDOLPH.) Didn't you say you thought he was alone, standing by the side of the road, hitchhiking? What else would he be doing out there?

RANDOLPH: I may have. I don't remember.

HARRINGTON: (*To* RANDOLPH.) You never said that. "Hitchhiking."

OEDIPUS: (*To* HARRINGTON.) He should know what he said, shouldn't he?

HARRINGTON: He said he *may* have said that. "Hitchhiking." He said he couldn't remember.

OEDIPUS: Never mind, never mind! Let's get on with it. What happens next?

RANDOLPH: A car comes along.

OEDIPUS: A car.

RANDOLPH: Very slowly. From the east. Very heavy. Kind of greenish black.

OEDIPUS: Wait a minute, wait a minute. How do you know all these things? How do you know it was greenish black, for instance?

HARRINGTON: Paint chips.

OEDIPUS: (*To* HARRINGTON.) I'm not talking to you. I'm talking to him.

HARRINGTON: Yes, sir.

OEDIPUS: (*Back to* RANDOLPH.) How do you know all these things?

RANDOLPH: Well, the direction's easy. The trajectory of the tire tread. The weight is measured by the depth of the tracks. And the color—well, the color—

OEDIPUS: Yeah. How do you know the color?

RANDOLPH: Paint chips.

(OEDIPUS *looks quickly to* HARRINGTON, *then back to* RANDOLPH.)

OEDIPUS: (*To* RANDOLPH.) Then what? What time of day was it? Can you tell that from the evidence?

RANDOLPH: Yes, sir. Early morning?

OEDIPUS: And how do you know that?

RANDOLPH: Dew stains on the windshield, sir.

OEDIPUS: Oh, so you found the car, then?

RANDOLPH: Yes, sir. Abandoned at a liquor store in Cucamonga.

OEDIPUS: So you know what color the car was by the actual car. What is this bullshit about paint chips?

HARRINGTON: We found the paint chips before the car.

OEDIPUS: (*Turns on* HARRINGTON.) When I want information from you, I'll ask directly!

HARRINGTON: Yes, sir.

(*A transition begins to occur where* OEDIPUS *becomes more and more angry. He's limping around, head down.*

Jams the butt of the cigar between his teeth, getting belligerent. HARRINGTON *cringes slightly.* RANDOLPH *becomes silent and stiff.*)

OEDIPUS: (*Pacing, head down, with cigar.*) So there's a killer by the side of the road, hitchhiking. He's alone. A car comes slowly from the east. A big, heavy, greenish black car. By all accounts. Dew on the windshield. What happens next?

RANDOLPH: Well—

OEDIPUS: (*Keeps pacing.*) Go on.

RANDOLPH: The car starts inexplicably edging over onto the shoulder of the road.

OEDIPUS: The shoulder the lone man was hitchhiking on?

RANDOLPH: That's right.

OEDIPUS: Inexplicably?

RANDOLPH: Well, they're all alone on the desert out there. There's nobody around.

OEDIPUS: How many's in the car? This big, heavy, greenish black car?

RANDOLPH: Three, sir. One driver and the other two in back.

OEDIPUS: And so far, we don't really know who they are?

HARRINGTON: Oh, we know who they are, all right.

OEDIPUS: (*Turns on* HARRINGTON.) SHUT UP!!

HARRINGTON: Sorry, sir.

OEDIPUS: I meant at this point! At this point in time we don't know who they are. They could be anyone.

HARRINGTON: That's right.

RANDOLPH: They could be anyone. At this point in time. He's right.

OEDIPUS: It's not until something happens that it becomes a crime! Until someone gets killed! Right now they're all living and breathing! They're enjoying the desert air. As far as we know they might all be singing.

HARRINGTON: Singing?

OEDIPUS: The car seems to be almost floating. Edging over into the hitchhiker's line of vision. Inexplicably!

RANDOLPH: (*Catching some of* OEDIPUS's *mysterious excitement.*) Yes! That's right. And the hitchhiker doesn't seem to budge. He just stands his ground.

OEDIPUS: Why should he budge?

RANDOLPH: I don't know. So he doesn't get run over, I guess.

OEDIPUS: It's an empty desert. Plenty of room for everyone. Why should the hitchhiker budge? He's there first. The car can go around him, can't it?

RANDOLPH: Yes, of course. But—

OEDIPUS: The hitchhiker has every right to be there!

RANDOLPH: I suppose, but—

OEDIPUS: So he's the one in a vulnerable position, isn't he? Not them. He's the one who could be easily destroyed. Not them. He's the one who could be demolished. Eradicated from the earth! Wiped out in the blink of an eye.

RANDOLPH: Well, of course. But—

OEDIPUS: So what do you suppose happens?

RANDOLPH: How should I know?

OEDIPUS: You're the expert. Don't you see what's coming?

RANDOLPH: No!

OEDIPUS: The car comes to a stop and just sits there with the engine idling, the tinted windows rolled up and the three men inside just staring out the window. What's the hitchhiker do now?

RANDOLPH: I don't know.

OEDIPUS: He doesn't either. Anything could happen. There's a threat in the air! Isn't there?

RANDOLPH: A threat?

HARRINGTON: (*To* OEDIPUS.) Can you see the driver?

OEDIPUS: (*Slowly turns to* HARRINGTON.) Of course I can see the driver.

RANDOLPH: What's the driver doing?

OEDIPUS: (*To* RANDOLPH.) He gets out. At the same time the driver gets out, a back door opens and another guy gets out. They both leave the doors wide-open and the engine idling.

HARRINGTON: That means there's one guy left inside! In the backseat.

RANDOLPH: That had to have been Langos or Laius or— whatever you want to call him. The former king. The father of—

(*Long menacing pause as* OEDIPUS *limps very slowly and deliberately over to* RANDOLPH, *stops right up close to him, and takes ahold of his lapel.*)

OEDIPUS: (*In* RANDOLPH's *face.*) What'd you say?

RANDOLPH: That had to have been the king that was murdered. Inside the car. In the back.

OEDIPUS: (*Shifts into a deep, dark tone, backing* RANDOLPH *up slowly, clenching* RANDOLPH's *lapel.*) I'll tell you what happened. You want to know? You want to know what actually happened? (OEDIPUS *moves closer to* RANDOLPH, *more threatening.* RANDOLPH *backs up.*) The driver came right up to me and shoved his face into mine. Just like this. I could see my own face in the lenses of his dark glasses. My scrawny face, staring back at me. He asked me if there was something wrong and I told him, "No, nothing's wrong!" He asked me if there was something wrong with my foot. Why was one of my feet bigger than the other one? And I told him it swelled up like that because my father was afraid of me when I was a baby. Somebody had told him that when I grew up I was going to kill him. My father. Kill my very own father and sleep with my very own mother. So he bound up my ankles and drove a stake through the left one, then hung me in a tree upside down so I'd bleed to death. The driver snickered when I told him this. He turned to the man behind and gave him a wink. The other man didn't wink back. The driver turned to me again and told me I was in his way, that I should get off the road and let him pass. I told him there was plenty of room to get around me. This was a big country. There was room for everyone. And then do you know what he did? (RANDOLPH *shakes his head.*) He gave me a little shove. Like this. (OEDIPUS *pokes* RANDOLPH *sharply in the middle of the chest with his index finger.*) Right in the middle of the chest. Just like this. (*He pokes* RANDOLPH *again, who stumbles back.*)

HARRINGTON: Now, just a second.

OEDIPUS: (*To* HARRINGTON.) You stay out of this! (*Back to* RANDOLPH, *unrelenting.*) Then I ran to the car. The driver tried to stop me, but I knocked him down. The other guy pulled a gun, but I jumped in the car. It was still idling. A bullet crashed through the window as I got behind the wheel. I looked in the backseat. It was my father with a short cigar sticking out of his teeth. We looked into each other's eyes for just a second. Surprised. I remembered him. His eyes. He slammed the door open with his shoulder and ran. I punched the car in reverse and tried to catch him, but the driver had recovered, grabbing the hood ornament with both hands. So I dropped it down into first and ran over him. The other guy kept shooting. Bullets were ripping through the headliner and blasting through glass. So I drove straight for him and ran his ass down, too. Then I went hunting for my father. He was running across the desert with his tie flying. He'd lost one of his shoes, so now and then he would hop like an injured rabbit. Limping. Just like me. Limping. I caught up to him and ran him over from behind. Then I backed over his head. Smashed it like a melon. I remember the popping sound. I stopped and got out. I walked back to the body. I stepped on what was left of his face with my big left foot. Then I pissed all over his chest. Then I went back to the car and drove off in the direction of Cucamonga. (*He moves off in a daze toward down left.*) That's about all I can remember.

(*He exits left, leaving* HARRINGTON *and* RANDOLPH *bewildered. When* OEDIPUS *has gone, suddenly, an extremely loud crash as though a large crate full of china dishes has been dropped from a great height, off-stage. It's important that this sound effect has a "live" quality to it. At the same time,* ANTIGONE *screams and a white curtain falls from the ceiling and hangs there, extreme downstage. A large black silhouette of* JOCASTA, *hanged by her neck, falls and swings slowly, casting an image across the curtain. This all happens as simultaneously as possible.* HARRINGTON *and* RANDOLPH *run off in terror.* ANTIGONE *enters with a long, crooked walking stick, tapping it as she goes, as though blind. She seems almost catatonic as she wanders on, chanting the word "Mama" in a kind of incantation. She keeps it up continuously as the silhouette of* JOCASTA *continues to slowly swing.* OEDIPUS *comes on behind the curtain, limping toward the silhouette, offstage. A horrible, grief-stricken moan comes from* OEDIPUS *as he encounters the corpse of* JOCASTA. *In silhouette we see* OEDIPUS *embrace the corpse, then leave it swinging as he comes onstage, his eyes streaming with blood.* ANTIGONE *keeps wandering and repeating "Mama" under* OEDIPUS. *The corpse keeps swinging.)*

Scene 32

OEDIPUS: The queen—my mother, my bride. All the great days, like ghosts, gone. Gone. The horrors of my own doing. Blind—blind to those for whom I was searching. All is wailing and ruin now. All. How can I bear to see when all my sight is horror. Everywhere. Night. Gone. My father. My sister. My daughter. My child. (ANTIGONE *takes his hand and places the long, crooked walking stick in it. He leans on it, becoming ancient.* ANTIGONE *takes his other hand and begins leading him.*) My faithful daughter. Lead me. Lead me away. I am sick. Sick in daily life. Sick in my origins. Take me away.

(ANTIGONE *leads him slowly off, continuing to chant "Mama" softly to herself.* OEDIPUS *hobbles along, clutching his walking stick, very old. As they both exit behind the white curtain, their shadows are cast up along with the swinging corpse of* JOCASTA. TRAVELER *comes on down left as the* ORACLE, *in front of the white curtain. He speaks directly to the audience, very simply.*)

Scene 33

ORACLE: The whole city went back to being what it had always been—just a place where people came and went; births, lives, deaths. On the surface they seemed returned to health and self-confidence, but a distant memory still persisted, a shadow that never left. Something had been torn apart from the inside out. A ghost of something close at hand yet far enough away and so terrible as to pretend it never happened.

(ANTIGONE's *background repetition of "Mama" suddenly stops.* JOCASTA's *body continues to slowly swing as lights go to black.*)

BURIED CHILD

A revised edition of an American classic, Sam Shepard's Pulitzer Prize–winning *Buried Child* is as fierce and unforgettable as it was when it was first produced. A scene of madness greets Vince and his girlfriend as they arrive at the squalid farmhouse of Vince's hard-drinking grandparents, who seem to have no idea who he is. Nor does his father, Tilden, a hulking former all-American footballer, or his uncle, who has lost one of his legs to a chain saw. Only the memory of an unwanted child, buried in an undisclosed location, can hope to deliver this family.

Drama

HEARTLESS

When Roscoe, a sixty-five-year-old Cervantes scholar, runs off with a young woman named Sally, he decides to stay awhile in her family home. Soon he discovers that Sally's house—once inhabited by James Dean and perched precariously over the San Fernando Valley—is filled with secrets, sadness, and haunted women who cannot leave themselves or anyone else in peace. From Lucy, Sally's suspicious sister, to Mable, their Shakespeare-quoting invalid mother, to Elizabeth, Mable's lovely and mysteriously mute nurse, the forces of the house conspire to make Roscoe question his assumptions about everything. As scars and histories are revealed, Shepard shows, as only he can, what happens when the secrets simmering within a family boil over. *Heartless* masterfully explores the irrevocability of our pasts—and the possibility of life begun anew.

Drama

THE LATE HENRY MOSS, EYES FOR CONSUELA,
WHEN THE WORLD WAS GREEN

These three plays by Pulitzer Prize winner Sam Shepard
are bold, explosive, and ultimately redemptive dramas
propelled by family secrets and illuminated by a searching
intelligence. In *The Late Henry Moss*—which premiered in
San Francisco, starring Sean Penn and Nick Nolte—two
estranged brothers confront the past as they piece together
the drunken fishing expedition that preceded their father's
death. In *Eyes for Consuela*, based on Octavio Paz's classic story "The Blue Bouquet," a vacationing American
encounters a knife-toting Mexican bandit on a gruesome
quest. And in *When the World Was Green*, cowritten with
Joseph Chaikin, a journalist in search of her father inter-
views an old man who resolved a generations-old vendetta
by murdering the wrong man. Together, these plays form a
powerful trio from an enduring force in American theater.

Drama

ALSO AVAILABLE

Cruising Paradise
Day out of Days
Fifteen One-Act Plays
The God of Hell
Great Dream of Heaven
Kicking a Dead Horse
States of Shock, Far North, Silent Tongue
Simpatico
Tooth of Crime

VINTAGE BOOKS
Available wherever books are sold.
www.vintagebooks.com